Muff and Ruff

by Bobby Lynn Maslen
pictures by John R. Maslen

Scholastic Inc.

New York • Toronto • London • Auckland • Sydney • Mexico City • New Delhi • Hong Kong • Buenos Aires

Beginning sounds for Book 8:

U u – umbrella

F f – feather

Ask for Bob Books at your local bookstore, or visit www.bobbooks.com.

ISBN 0-545-02721-7

6 5 4 3 2 1   7 8 9 10 11/0

Printed in China
This edition first printing, September 2007

Muff and Ruff tug a rag rug.

Mac ran to Ruff.

Mac, Muff, and Ruff tug.

Rip it up, Ruff.

Nip at it, Muff.

Ruff hid in it.

Muff and Mac sat on it.

A rag rug is fun for
Muff, Ruff, and Mac.

The End

Available Bob Books®:

Set 1: Beginning Readers — With consistent new sounds added gradually, your new reader is gently introduced to all the letters of the alphabet. They can soon say, "I read the whole book!®"

Set 2: Advancing Beginners — The use of three-letter words and consistent vowel sounds in slightly longer stories build skill and confidence.

Set 3: Word Families — Consonant blends, endings and a few sight words advance reading skills while the use of word families keep reading manageable.

Set 4: Compound Words — Longer books and complex words engage young readers as proficiency advances.

Set 5: Long Vowels — Silent *e* and other vowel blends build young readers' vocabulary and aptitude.

Bob Books® Collections:

Collection 1 — Includes Set 1: Beginning Readers and part of Set 2: Advancing Beginners

Collection 2 — Includes part of Set 2: Advancing Beginners and Set 3: Word Families

Collection 3 — Includes Set 4: Compound Words and Set 5: Long Vowels